Pumpkin Fiesta

BY CARYN YACOWITZ

ILLUSTRATED BY JOE CEPEDA

■ HARPERCOLLINSPUBLISHERS

The inspiration for *Pumpkin Fiesta* came from "The Stub-Book,"
a story by the nineteenth century Spanish writer Pedro Antonio de Alarcón.

The art in this book was created using oil paint on illustration board.

Pumpkin Fiesta
Text copyright © 1998 by Caryn Yacowitz
Illustraions copyright © 1998 by Joe Cepeda
Printed in the U.S.A. All rights reserved.
http://www.harperchildrens.com
Library of Congress Cataloging-in-Publication Data
Yacowitz, Caryn.
    Pumpkin fiesta / by Caryn Yacowitz ; illustrated by Joe Cepeda.
        p.   cm.
    Summary: Hoping to win a prize for the best pumpkin at the fiesta, Foolish Fernando tries to copy
Old Juana's successful gardening techniques, but without really watching to see how much effort and
love she puts into her work. Includes a recipe for pumpkin soup.
    ISBN 0-06-027658-4
    [1. Pumpkin—Fiction.   2. Mexico—Fiction.]   I. Cepeda, Joe, ill.   II. Title.
PZ7.Y126Pu   1998   96-48580
[E]—dc21   CIP
                                                                                            AC

Typography by Al Cetta
1 2 3 4 5 6 7 8 9 10
❖
First Edition

For Jerry and for Mike, with love
—C.Y.

In memory of Helen Sandoval and
Juanita Talavera Flores
—J.C.

Old Juana grew the biggest, roundest, and orangest pumpkins in the whole province of San Miguel. For as long as anyone could remember, she had won the special pumpkin crown at the big *fiesta* each year.

Everyone in her village was proud of Old Juana. All except her neighbor, Foolish Fernando.

"I will discover Old Juana's secret, and this year my pumpkins will be the finest at the *fiesta*," Fernando boasted to his pet bull, Toro.

At planting time Fernando followed Old Juana to Pumpkin Hill and hid behind a bush. He watched as Juana and her little burro, Dulcita, plowed the field. Old Juana broke up the clods of soil with her hoe until they crumbled like fresh cake in her hands.

Her faded cotton dress fluttered in the cool spring breeze. Her big straw hat cast a pool of shadow on the freshly tilled soil. Old Juana bent so low that her chin almost touched her knees as she carefully planted plump, white pumpkin seeds—one, two, three to a mound.

Foolish Fernando watched and watched. Then he ran home as fast as his skinny legs could carry him.

Early the next day Fernando began hoeing his plot of land. He wore a faded cotton dress and a big straw hat. He quickly scattered seeds in every direction.

"I looked just like Old Juana today," Foolish Fernando said, scratching Toro behind the ears. "I'm sure that is the secret to her pumpkins."

Soon the warm spring rains came. The vines on Old Juana's Pumpkin Hill grew strong. Their twisting tendrils hugged the ground.

Fernando looked at his scrawny vines. Could there be another secret? he wondered.

The next morning when Old Juana and Dulcita passed by, carrying heavy jugs of water from the well, Fernando left his favorite spot in the pepper tree and followed them to Pumpkin Hill.

"*Agua, agua.* Water, water, my beauties." Old Juana's words carried on the warm wind as she gave each plant a cool drink. "Butter babies, butter babies," she cooed to each yellow blossom. "Open your faces to the sun, invite the honey bees to visit you. Soon you will grow to be fat, round pumpkins."

"¡*Si*! ¡*Si*! Yes! Yes!" Fernando cried. When he got home, he put on the faded cotton dress and his straw hat. Fernando scooped some water into an old clay pot. He ran back to Pumpkin Hill.

"*Agua, agua,*" he called. "Water, water, my beauties." He splashed a few drops of water on his plants. "Baby butters, butter balls, buttercups." A drop of water landed here, another splashed there. "Big butters, baby cups, butter-ups," Fernando said. He talked to his pumpkins until the sun set.

Before he went to bed, Fernando danced a little jig. "I know the secret of Pumpkin Hill," he told Toro. "I looked like Old Juana and talked like her, too! I will wear the pumpkin crown this year!"

All the long, hot summer Old Juana and Dulcita carried water to Pumpkin Hill. The yellow blossoms turned into baby pumpkins. A few grew to be as large and as round as wagon wheels. Old Juana named her three finest pumpkins Gorda, who was the chubbiest, Linda, the prettiest, and Blush Bottom, for her color.

Fernando talked to his plants, but he often forgot to water them. Only a few blossoms turned into small, green pumpkins. "Something is not right," he said. "I will watch Old Juana one last time."

Fernando ran to Pumpkin Hill and hid. He watched as Old Juana and Dulcita carefully picked insects off the vines.

"*¡Por supuesto!* Of course!" he cried. "Why didn't I see it before? Toro will have to help me."

The next morning Fernando gathered straw and twine. He went to his field, pulling Toro behind him.

Foolish Fernando plucked one hungry bug from one leaf. Toro stood near him, embarrassed; his head hung low.

"Well done," declared Fernando that evening. "I know all the secrets now. I looked and talked just like Old Juana, and you, my precious pet, looked just like Dulcita! I'm sure my pumpkins will be the finest at the *fiesta*!"

But Toro charged away to the farthest corner of the field and did not come back, even at midnight.

By autumn Old Juana's biggest pumpkins—Gorda, Linda, and Blush Bottom—had all turned the color of the harvest moon. Fernando's pumpkins were small, shriveled, and green.

The night before the *fiesta* Fernando crept among the vines of Pumpkin Hill. With a whack and a chop he cut Gorda, Linda, and Blush Bottom from their vines and heaved them into his cart.

At dawn on *fiesta* day Old Juana and Dulcita arrived at Pumpkin Hill. Old Juana looked at the spot where her beautiful pumpkins had grown. She could not believe her eyes. "Where are my children?" she cried. "Who has stolen my beauties?"

She searched every corner of Pumpkin Hill.

When she was sure they were nowhere to be found, Old Juana took a knife and bent over the vines where Gorda, Linda, and Blush Bottom had grown.

With heavy hearts Old Juana and Dulcita traveled the dusty road to the *fiesta*.

When they arrived, they heard music and cheering. Pushing through the crowd, Old Juana spied Gorda, Linda, and Blush Bottom. There, sitting proudly behind them, grinned Foolish Fernando! The mayor held the pumpkin crown over Fernando's head.

"Stop! Stop!" Old Juana cried. The music ceased. The crowd was silent. All eyes were on Old Juana.

"Those are my pumpkins!" she cried. A look of shock spread through the crowd.

"What proof do you have that these are your pumpkins?" asked the mayor.

"I tilled the soil and planted the seeds on Pumpkin Hill. I carried water to the plants every day. I removed the insects that ate the leaves," Juana replied.

"Perhaps so," said the mayor, "but you must show us proof."

"The pumpkins are mine," said Juana. "I can prove it." She reached deep into her pocket and pulled out the stubs of the vines where each pumpkin had been cut. "Here is Gorda's. And Linda's— see how it fits her like a little cap. And this one belongs to my precious Blush Bottom."

A murmur swept the crowd. "These are indeed Old Juana's pumpkins!" shouted the mayor. He placed the crown on Old Juana's head.

The crowd let out a roar.

"*¡Viva Juana! ¡Viva Juana!*" they chanted. "Long live Juana! Long live Juana!"

Foolish Fernando was about to sneak away when the mayor scooped him up and brought him to Old Juana.

Fernando stood before her, his head bent low.

"I'm sorry, Juana," said Fernando. "I was wrong to take your pumpkins."

"Foolish, Foolish Fernando," said Old Juana. "Do you really want to grow beautiful, big pumpkins?"

"*¡Si! ¡Si!*" shouted Fernando.

"Will you pay attention and do as I say?" asked Old Juana.

"*¡Si! ¡Si! Te prometo!* Yes! Yes! I promise you!" shouted Fernando.

"Well," said Old Juana with a smile, "then I will teach you."

And Old Juana taught Foolish Fernando the secret of Pumpkin Hill.

OLD JUANA'S RECIPE FOR PUMPKIN SOUP IN A PUMPKIN

6 cups chicken broth or vegetable broth

4–5 cups pared pumpkin, cut into $\frac{1}{2}$-inch cubes

1 cup thinly sliced onion

2 cloves minced garlic

1 teaspoon dried thyme leaves

5 peppercorns

$\frac{1}{2}$ cup low-fat milk, warmed

1 tablespoon freshly chopped parsley

$\frac{1}{8}$ cup toasted, shelled pumpkin seeds

In a covered saucepan heat all ingredients except milk, parsley, and pumpkin seeds to boiling. Reduce heat; simmer uncovered for 40 minutes. Transfer pumpkin mixture to a large bowl. In a blender or food processor puree the pumpkin mixture in batches. Return pureed mixture to saucepan. Heat to boiling; reduce heat. Simmer uncovered for 10 minutes.

Stir warmed milk into soup. Serve hot in a hollowed-out pumpkin that has been warmed 20 minutes in a 350°F oven. Garnish with parsley and toasted pumpkin seeds.

SERVES 8

Old Juana—and Foolish Fernando—think this soup is delicious!